MW01641265

The Adventures of
Goliath

Goliath at the Seaside

The Adventures of
David and Goliath

Goliath at the Seaside

Terrance Dicks
Illustrated by
Valerie Littlewood

New York

First edition for the United States and the Philippines published 1989 by
Barron's Educational Series, Inc.

First published 1988 by Piccadilly Press Ltd., London, England

All inquiries should be addressed to:
Barron's Educational Series, Inc.
250 Wireless Boulevard
Hauppauge, New York 11788

Library of Congress Catalog Card No. 88-7764
International Standard Book No. 0-8120-4209-3

Library of Congress Cataloging-in-Publication Data

Dicks, Terrance.
Goliath at the seaside/Terrance Dicks; illustrated by Valerie Littlewood.
p. cm — (The adventures of Goliath)
Summary: David and his big dog, Goliath, solve a mystery involving stinging seaweed and illegal toxic dumping at a seaside resort.
ISBN 0-8120-4209-3
[1. Mystery and detective stories. 2. Dogs—Fiction. 3. Water-Pollution—Fiction.] I. Littlewood, Valerie, ill. II. Title. III. Series: Dicks, Terrance. Adventures of Goliath.
PZ7.D5627Gtu 1989
E—dc19 88-7764
CIP
AC

PRINTED IN THE UNITED STATES OF AMERICA
012 9770 987654321

CONTENTS

Chapter One

Trouble on the Beach

"Two vanilla cones please," said David. "And one with sprinkles!"

"I can guess who that one's for," said the beach shop lady.

David grinned. "Well, I deserve it, don't I? I'm doing all the fetching and carrying. Mom and Dad are just lazing on the beach."

The beach shop lady, a large and motherly woman called Mrs. Meggs, started to get the ice cream. "Back again, dear?"

Like most grown-ups, she had a habit of saying the obvious.

David felt like answering. "No, I'm just an optical illusion!" But he was fond of Mrs. Meggs, so he just said, "That's right, back again."

Mr. Meggs came out of the kitchen and starting making cold cuts for the lunchtime rush. He was small and jolly—unlike his wife who was large and jolly—and they'd both known David since he was quite small. David and his family had been coming to this little seaside resort, on and off, for several years. "Where's Goliath?"

"Goliath's around somewhere," said David. "He got delayed by some little kids on the beach—he was giving them rides!"

As he spoke, Goliath, David's dog, rushed into the shop like a great hairy

whirlwind, and put his feet up on the counter. Goliath was a very big dog indeed, bigger than David when he stood on his hind legs.

Mr. Meggs tossed him a scrap of

beef. "Doesn't get any smaller, does he?"

Mrs. Meggs put the three ice creams— two vanilla cones and one extra large cone with chocolate sprinkles —into a special holder on the counter. "There you are, dear."

David gave her the money and scooped the ice cream up.

Goliath gave a loud woof and looked expectantly at Mrs. Meggs.

She laughed. "I know what you want!"

She took a piece of candy from a jar on the counter and tossed it to Goliath who snapped it up in mid-air.

He woofed again, and Mrs. Meggs reached for another candy.

"Only one please," said David firmly. "He loves sweets, but they're not really good for him."

"That's right," said Mrs. Meggs.

"Don't want to stunt his growth, do we? Have a little more beef, boy."

He tossed Goliath another piece of beef, Goliath snapped it up, and David and Goliath went out of the shop.

The beach shop was no more than a big hut on the edge of the parking lot. As well as things to eat and drink—tea, coffee, soft drinks, candy, ice cream, sandwiches, hamburgers and hot dogs —it sold just about everything else you could want for a day on the beach. Sunglasses, suntan oil, kites and rubber rafts, wind shelters, surfboards, beach balls—the list was endless.

The beach shop, the parking lot and the beach itself were more or less all there was to Sandy Bay, which was why David's parents like it so much.

Sandy Bay itself lived up to its name

—a little bay scooped out of the coastline, with safe swimming and a rim of low, easily-climbed cliffs.

There was a little village a mile inland, and there were bigger resorts with many shops and small cafés and entertainment not far away, but at Sandy Bay there was the beach shop and the beach and that was it. David's parents rented the same vacation cottage year after year, usually in the early part of the summer, before things got too crowded.

David hurried across the parking lot and then across the beach, though it was hard to hurry on soft sand.

By the time he reached his parents, melted ice cream had started to dribble down his arms.

"Good old Sandy Bay," said David's dad, licking his ice cream. "Never changes, does it?"

"That's what's so nice about it," said David's mom. "This is exactly the kind of seaside vacation I had when I was young!"

But something had changed about Sandy Bay. And it was a change very much for the worse.

Actually, it was Goliath who made the discovery.

He was trotting up and down at the edge of the sea, making cautious little dashes in and out of the waves.

Goliath wasn't all that excited about sea swimming. He was a bit timid, in spite of his great size, and he didn't like it at all when the big waves splashed him.

Suddenly Goliath began barking at something he'd found on the shore.

"What's upsetting him now?" asked David's mother.

His father said, "Who knows? The

last time he was being attacked by a savage crab!"

To a dog with Goliath's nervous nature, the beach was full of unknown dangers.

"Seems to be just a clump of seaweed," said David. "I'll go and take a look!"

He trotted to the water's edge, and found Goliath sniffing suspiciously at a big chunk of seaweed.

As David approached, Goliath looked up and barked.

David squatted down and looked at the seaweed. "It's only seaweed, you big baby. Seaweed can't hurt you."

Goliath barked again as if he wasn't convinced.

David studied the seaweed.

It was certainly very nasty-looking seaweed, and it was of a kind he hadn't seen before—a big, slimy

purple splodge of it.

There seemed to be something caught underneath it.

He reached out and moved the weed a little, shuddering at its slimy feel. Something silvery floated free.

It was a dead fish.

"Yuk!" said David. "Come away, Goliath. Leave!"

David dragged Goliath back to his parents. "He found a piece of smelly old seaweed, with a dead fish in it."

"Trust Goliath," said David's mother sleepily.

David felt an odd tingling in his left index finger and thumb, and waved them in the air. "Seem to have stung myself . . ."

Suddenly a toddler in a bathing suit came staggering up the beach, crying piteously.

"What's the matter?" asked David's mother.

"Leg . . ." sobbed the little girl. "Hurts!"

Sure enough, the little girl had an angry red patch on one chubby knee. A few strands of purple seaweed clung to the area.

The little girl's mother came running up, and they handed her over. As the sobbing child was carried away, David's mother said, "Poor little thing. She must have fallen and scraped her knee."

David said slowly, "I'm not so sure. Look!"

He held out his left hand. Finger and thumb were an angry red—just like the little girl's knee. "It's where I touched that seaweed Goliath found—and there was a bit of the same stuff on that kid's knee. That purple seaweed—it must be poisonous!"

David jumped to his feet, borrowed a shovel from a startled kid building a sand castle, scooped up the smelly chunk of seaweed and buried it in a hole in the sand. "That's the end of that!"

His father said gently, "I'm afraid not, son. Look!" He pointed. To his horror, David saw that there were chunks of the purple weed drifting in all along the beach . . .

Chapter Two

The Poison Weed

David looked at the weed in amazement. "What are we going to do?"

His father scratched his head. "I don't really see what we can do."

"Should we report it to the police?"

"Well, they can't come and arrest a lot of seaweed, can they?"

"David's right, though," said his mother. "We ought to report it to somebody—the local town board, or someone like that!"

"Well, let's see what things are like tomorrow," said his father. "Maybe the tide'll wash it all away!"

They collected their beach stuff and went back to the cottage.

That night they drove to the nearby seaside town for a meal out and a walk along the main street, so David didn't see any more of the beach that day.

As he fell asleep he was telling himself that his father was right, that next day the tide would have carried the weed away . . .

The next day, David began nagging everyone into getting down to the beach bright and early, hoping desperately that the weed had gone away. But it hadn't. It had returned in force.

The slimy purple splodges seemed to be everywhere, deposited in clumps on the beach by the out-going tide.

There was even a sort of floating line of the stuff along the water's edge, so that you had to wade through it to get to the clear water beyond.

Before long the beach started to fill up and very soon the air was full of the yells of weed-stung children and the grumbles of their angry parents.

The effect of the stinging weed wasn't really all that bad. David's reddened fingers had returned to normal overnight, helped a great deal by a dab of soothing cream, and he took care not to touch the stuff again. Adults seemed to get away with just a sort of itching rash. It was the little kids who really caught it, all the toddlers stumbling around with their buckets and shovels.

David and his parents did their best to warn people, but there were far too many families around to warn them all. People started packing up and clearing off, and by lunchtime the beach was almost deserted.

David and his family decided to go too, especially when Goliath sniffed a big clump of weed and got his nose stung. He yelped pathetically for ages, and by the time they'd got him soothed they were all fed up.

"Let's go and have a quick snack in the beach shop," said David's father. "Then we'll drive down the coast a bit, find somewhere cleaner . . ."

Usually the beach shop was crowded at lunchtime, but there were only a few people in there today, all grumbling about the invasion of the purple weed.

Mr. and Mrs. Meggs were far from their usual cheerful selves as they served David and his family tea and pastry. "Worst day's business I've had for years," grumbled Mr. Meggs.

"That's right," said Mrs. Meggs. "Just when it looked like it was going to be a really good summer."

"It's disgraceful," said an angry-looking man. "All this pollution, that's what it is, people dump

anything in the sea these days . . ."

A high, clear voice came from the doorway. "That's right my good fellow. And we all know who's been dumping stuff into Sandy Bay"

A tall, white-haired old lady was standing in the doorway. She had a beaky nose with glasses perched on the end, and piercing blue eyes. She was wearing a hairy tweed coat and skirt, and she carried a walking stick.

"Now then, Miss Grimes, what are you talking about?" said Mr. Meggs. But he didn't sound any too sure of himself.

"I'm talking about you dumping rubbish into the creek behind your café, my man," said Miss Grimes. "You needn't bother to deny it, I've seen you through my binoculars. And I've got photographic proof as well!"

She marched into the shop and

threw a photograph down on the counter.

Everyone crowded to look at it, David at the front. The photograph

had been taken from some distance, probably through a telephoto lens, but it was clear enough. It showed Mr. Meggs, tipping the contents of an overflowing bin into the little tidal creek that ran behind the shop.

"I will be sending a copy of that photograph to the town board," said Miss Grimes triumphantly. "We'll see what they have to say about it." She turned and marched out of the shop.

"Well," said the angry-looking man. "Now we know who to blame, don't we?"

He put down his unfinished tea and marched right out of the shop and the others followed him.

David and Goliath and David's parents stayed on, largely because they felt so sorry for poor Mr. Meggs.

"Who was that?" asked David.

Mr. Meggs sighed. "Miss Grimes is

president of the Sandy Bay Residents' Association. She has that big house up on the cliffs. She never wanted a beach shop here in the first place. She opposed it at the town meeting. Now she thinks she's got a good chance of closing me down. Not only am I losing all my trade, now I'm going to get the blame for it as well!"

David looked at the photograph.

"Yes, I did throw stuff in the creek now and then," said Mr. Meggs angrily. "And I know I'm not supposed to. But it was only food waste from the café—potato peel, bread crusts and stuff like that. The tide takes it away and the crabs and fish eat it."

"The garbage bins get full to overflowing when we're busy," said Mrs. Meggs. "Food waste goes bad and it smells if you don't get rid of it, especially in hot weather, and I was afraid it wasn't healthy."

"If the town would empty those bins a bit more often . . ." grumbled Mr. Meggs. "Still, what's the use, it's done now."

David's mother finished her tea. "Well, we'd better be on our way. I hope it all gets cleared up, Mr. Meggs. Come on, David."

David shook his head. "No, you two go. Go and visit a nice monument or museum or something. Goliath and I are staying here."

His father looked puzzled. "Whatever for? What are you going to do?"

"Oh, we'll just wander around Sandy Bay," said David.

It took a little longer to convince them, but eventually they left, leaving David a key to the cottage so he could get in if he wanted to, and some money for food at the café.

As soon as his parents had gone, David turned to Mr. Meggs. "Right, this is where I need your help. I need a local map, supplies of food and drink for the afternoon and something to carry it all in . . . I'd better have a compass as well, please."

Mr. Meggs said, "Well, I reckon we can find all that for you. Are you going exploring?"

"I'm planning a scientific expedition," said David. "I don't think your kitchen rubbish is responsible for that weed, Mr. Meggs. I don't see how it could be. You've been throwing in potato peel, not dumping atomic waste."

Mrs. Meggs looked puzzled and hopeful at the same time. "So what did cause it, then?"

"I don't know," said David. "Not yet anyway. But we're going to find out—aren't we, Goliath?"

Goliath woofed his agreement.

Chapter Three

The Sinister Farm

Ten minutes later, David was on his way out of the café, a large sack full of supplies and provisions on his back. The Meggses had insisted on providing everything he needed without charge. As they'd said, at the moment David and Goliath seemed to be the only ones on their side.

As they crossed the parking lot, a white police car drew up and a very large, very young policeman got out.

It was Officer Penberry, Archie to his friends, who lived in the police house in the village with his wife and baby son. He nodded to David, and made a fuss over Goliath who barked a welcome. "Morning, young David."

"Morning," said David. "What brings you down here?"

"We had a complaint, about illegal disposal of garbage."

"I can guess who from," said David, and told him about the scene in the beach shop.

Archie shaded his eyes with his hand and looked along the beach. "It's rather a mess," he said. "Doesn't seem likely a few food scraps could cause all that."

"That's what I think," said David. "Has there been any oil spillage or chemical pollution out at sea?"

Archie shook his head. "First thing I

checked on. No reports at all. Besides it'd have to be going on for some time you know. That's why things look so bad for old Meggs."

"Are there any factories or chemical works or anything like that around here?" asked David hopefully.

"No there's not, nor atomic power stations either. It's all farming around here, farming and tourism."

Goliath woofed impatiently, and David said goodbye and went on his way.

David was thinking hard as he and Goliath walked along the beach and picked their way between the clumps of weed.

If the pollution wasn't coming from the sea it must be coming from the land. In the kind of science fiction movie you saw on TV it was always atomic waste that was the culprit—

that or some mad scientist who liked to experiment with strange chemicals. Since there didn't seem to be any atomic places around, he'd just have to keep his eye open for mad scientists, David decided.

If you stood facing the water, the beach shop and parking lot were on the far right hand side of the bay, and David had decided to cross the bay from one side to the other, looking for clues.

As he walked along, it was clear that the clumps of weed were getting bigger and more frequent, which made David feel he must be heading in the right direction.

Goliath trotted along beside him enjoying the walk, though he took care to avoid the clumps of weed. It must have stung his nose badly when he sniffed it, thought David.

The curve of the bay ended in a big headland, a towering hill with a church on top. You could climb up to it by a winding path. Just under the hill a tiny river ran down to the sea, with a narrow footbridge across so you could go on walking along the coast.

David paused on the bridge and looked down.

The shallow water below was thick

with the purple weed, a sort of bed of it.

David went on his way, and very soon he noticed something else. The weed was thinning out . . .

Frowning, David retraced his steps.

Crossing the bridge again, he went down to the borders of the little river.

Goliath followed him, sniffed at the cloudy water and whined.

David sniffed the water too. His sense of smell wasn't as good as Goliath's of course—but wasn't there some faint chemical smell?

David decided there was only one thing to do. He must follow the little river to its source.

Checking his bearings with map and compass, he set off.

It wasn't an easy journey.

The river bank was thickly grown with weeds, and you could hardly see the little riverside track for most of the time.

The weeds seemed particularly

dense and thick. They were extra tall as well, so that quite ordinary plants like reeds seemed to have shot up like trees.

David sent Goliath ahead as a sort of trail breaker, and the big dog crashed excitedly through the overgrown weeds, leaving a trail of flattened plants behind him. It struck David that the weeds were somehow feeble as well as tall—it was surprisingly easy to trample them out of your way.

Goliath crashed ahead, sometimes disappearing completely, so that David could only see his waving tail.

Suddenly the tail stopped waving and Goliath let out a series of crashing barks. David recognized it as his "Come and help me" signal.

Clearly Goliath had come across some obstacle.

David hurried up to join him, and

found that the obstacle in question was a rusty barbed wire fence that ran across the path. In front of it was a sign. It read:

Underneath the printed lettering someone had scrawled, "Trespassers will be SHOT!"

David frowned, and took out his map and studied it.

The marking was quite clear.

According to the map the riverside track was a public footpath.

David was an avid observer of the laws, and normally he wouldn't have dreamed of trespassing, but this, he decided, was a special case. But how was he going to get through the wire?

David studied the problem for a while. Not through, he decided, and certainly not over. But under? Maybe that was a possibility . . .

Fishing in his sack, David produced one of those camping sets—knife, fork and spoon held together in a metal clip. Using the knife to dig with and the spoon to clear away the soil, David started digging a hole in the soft earth below the bottom strand of wire, just to the left of the path.

Goliath sat watching him, puzzled, head cocked to one side. Digging was one of the things that had gotten him in trouble in the past, and now here was David digging a hole of his own.

Barking enthusiastically he joined in to help.

"Sssh! you big lummox," said David. "Just keep out of the way and leave this to me!"

Goliath looked hurt, but did as he was told.

When the hole looked big enough, David found the hard work had made him hungry. Mrs. Meggs had insisted on packing sandwiches, turnovers and doughnuts in the sack, together with a bottle of lemonade. There was far too much food for David, so he shared it with Goliath, who wolfed it down happily. Goliath could dispose of a whole sandwich in two bites.

When the picnic was finished, David put all the litter into the sack and hid it in a clump of bushes. Diving onto

his stomach he wriggled through the hole and under the wire, then pulled the lowest strand up so Goliath could follow. Goliath just about managed it, though he lost a bit of fur.

Holding Goliath by the collar, David began to creep down the path toward the farm . . .

Chapter Four

The Secret of Sandy Bay Farm

The path led through scruffy-looking fields full of straggly overgrown-looking crops. Buildings appeared—open-sided sheds with a farmhouse beyond.

Crouching low, David moved toward them.

There were rusty iron drums piled in the sheds, great big ones like the ones you used for gas or oil.

As David came nearer he smelled the same strange odor in the air that he'd smelled in the stream, though it was much stronger here. David moved closer, right up to the nearest stack of drums. One lay on its side with a trickle of fluid coming from the open cap. Goliath sniffed it and backed away, sneezing.

David dipped the tip of one finger into the liquid and sniffed it very cautiously.

It was the same smell as in the stream all right, and his finger was tingling.

"That's it!" said David out loud. "I remember now!"

Something that had been hovering at the back of his mind all day had suddenly become clear.

His mind went back to a long-ago geography lesson. Last term their teacher had told them about a natural, or rather unnatural, disaster that had happened in some other country, when suddenly the beaches had become covered in smelly weed. And he'd told them why . . .

A black shadow fell over him and a gruff voice growled, "And what might you be doing?"

David turned and looked up—and saw what looked like a giant towering over him.

The farmer—David guessed that must be who the man was—was a tremendously big and fat man with a bushy black beard. He wore a tweed hat like an upside-down flower pot, a tattered ski jacket, and grimy corduroys and massive boots.

He looked like the Giant when he catches Jack at the top of the beanstalk.

In his hand was a knobbly blackthorn stick. He shook it threateningly. "Well?"

Goliath barked and wagged his tail. The farmer glanced at him, then ignored him. "Well?" he said again. "What are you doing on my farm? Didn't you see the sign?"

"The one by the fence cutting off the public footpath?" said David boldly. "Yes, of course I saw it. I'm sorry if I'm trespassing, but I haven't done any damage to your farm. Besides, I'm investigating.

"Investigating what?"

"The weed that's spoiling the beach at Sandy Bay. The weed Mr. and Mrs. Meggs's shop is being blamed for—when it's all your fault!"

The farmer's face seemed to turn purple with rage. "Interfering little pest!" he roared. "As if I didn't have troubles enough!"

Almost mad with rage, he raised his stick to strike.

David looked to Goliath for help, but the big dog just barked happily and wagged his tail.

Suddenly David knew what Goliath was thinking. The big dog thought it was all a game and that the nice man had come to play with them.

As the club came down David shouted, "Fetch, Goliath! Fetch!"

With an excited bark, Goliath leaped up, snatched the blackthorn stick from the angry farmer's hand and galloped away with it!

The farmer yelled with rage and pounded after him. Tail wagging with delight, Goliath stepped up his speed.

David turned and shot off back down the path yelling, "This way, Goliath! Fetch!"

All three sped down the path in a sort of parade, David in the lead, Goliath next, the stick clamped in his jaws, and the farmer last.

Goliath was having the time of his life. He only really understood part of the game of "Fetch"—the part that involved *him* getting hold of the stick. At this point Goliath would run away, expecting the stick-thrower to chase him. He'd never really grasped the bit about bringing the stick back, and he was delighted to meet someone who knew how to play the game properly!

When David finally reached the hole beneath the fence he dived through it head-first, dragging himself through with his elbows. Then, wriggling around, he called, "Come on, Goliath!"

Still holding the stick, Goliath flopped down by the hole, but he made no attempt to come through. He was enjoying the game.

The farmer lumbered closer and

Goliath wagged his tail.

Suddenly David had an idea. Wriggling forward through the hole he grabbed the stick, one hand on each side of Goliath's jaws.

Since Goliath still refused to let go, David was able to use the stick as a sort of handle, tugging the big dog under the wire just in time.

The farmer panted up to the fence, then stopped, baffled by his own barbed wire. The hole, just big enough for David and Goliath, was far too small for him.

"You give me back my stick," he growled. "That's stealing, that is!"

"I'll hand it in to the police when I see them," said David. "Maybe they'll return it when they come around."

The farmer glared at him through the barbed wire. "Why should police be coming around here?"

"I think they'll have quite a few questions to ask you—mainly about where you got that fertilizer!"

David turned and ran off down the path, heading back toward the sea, and Goliath followed, the blackthorn stick still clamped firmly in his jaws.

This was certainly the best game of "Fetch" he and David had ever had!

"Fertilizer!" said David the next day. "The same thing happened in Sweden a few years ago. The farmers near the sea over-fertilized the land and the stuff seeped into the sea and fertilized the weeds. All the local beaches were ruined by smelly seaweed, just like here!"

With the help of Officer Penberry, David was explaining his triumphant investigation to an admiring audience in the Meggs's beach shop.

"You mean old Seth Bowman caused all this trouble by himself?" asked Mrs. Meggs wonderingly.

"But it was no ordinary fertilizer," explained David. "It was a special experimental batch that the company had decided not to go ahead with.

Trouble was it worked too well. Made the crops shoot up fast and then sort of collapse. It increased acidity too, that's why the weed stung people. I guessed it was something like that when I saw the weeds along the stream and the crops on that farm. They looked sort of unnatural."

"So how did this farmer of yours get hold of it?" asked David's father.

Officer Penberry explained.

"It seems when the fertilizer company decided to abandon the experiment, they gave the remains of their stock to a specialist contractor to be disposed of—there are strict rules about chemical waste. Unfortunately the contractor wasn't too honest. He saw the chance to make a few bucks by selling off his 'Super-fertilizer' cheap, and Seth Bowman was tempted."

David said, "And when the stuff ruined all the crops on his farm he started dumping it in the stream, the one that runs down to Sandy Bay. He confessed it all to Officer Penberry here when he went around to return his stick!"

"You had a lucky escape, if you ask me," said David's mother. "Trust you and Goliath to find trouble!"

"I won't hear a word against either of them," said Mr. Meggs. "Saved my bacon they have, and my meat pies and turnovers too. There's a free ice cream for you, young man, any time you come in my shop—and a meat pie for Goliath too!"

David felt embarrassed by all the praise—unlike Goliath who loved it. "Well, I think I'll take a walk on the beach and see how the clearing up's getting along." The town board had mounted a big operation to clear the weed. "Come on, Goliath!"

There weren't many kids on the beach yet, but there were one or two local residents were taking a stroll.

David saw a military-looking old gentleman marching briskly toward them waving a walking stick.

Goliath saw the man too—and the stick! He cocked his head. Maybe the man would like a game . . .

He trotted toward the old fellow, and suddenly David realized what Goliath was thinking.

"No!" he yelled but it was too late.

Galloping up to the astonished old gentleman, Goliath quickly snatched his walking stick and dashed away.

"Hey, come back!" yelled the startled old gentleman, setting off after him.

"Oh no," groaned David, running after them both.

Goliath trotted happily along the sands, listening to the shouts and yells of his two playmates. This, he thought, was one of the best vacations

he'd ever had!

Other *Adventures of Goliath* that you will enjoy reading:

Goliath and the Burglar
Goliath and the Buried Treasure
Goliath at the Dog Show
Goliath Goes to Summer School
Goliath on Vacation
Goliath's Christmas
Goliath's Easter Parade

About the author

After studying at Cambridge, Terrance Dicks became an advertising copywriter, then a radio and television scriptwriter and script editor. His career as a children's author began with the *Dr Who* series and he has now written a variety of other books on subjects ranging from horror to detection.

More Fun, Mystery, And Adventure With Goliath–

Goliath And The Burglar
The first Goliath story tells how David persuades his parents to buy him a puppy. When Goliath grows very big it appears that he might have to leave the household. David is worried—until a burglar enters the house, and Goliath becomes a hero! (Paperback, ISBN 3820-7—Library Binding, ISBN 5823-2)

Goliath And The Buried Treasure
When Goliath discovers how much fun it is to dig holes, both he and David get into trouble with the neighbors. Meanwhile, building developers have plans that will destroy the city park—until Goliath's skill at digging transforms him into the most unlikely hero in town! (Paperback, ISBN 3819-3—Library Binding, ISBN 5822-4)

Goliath On Vacation
David persuades his parents to bring Goliath with them on vacation—but the big hound quickly disrupts life at the hotel. Goliath is in trouble with David's parents, but he soon redeems himself when he helps David solve the mystery of the disappearing ponies. (Paperback, ISBN 3821-5—Library Binding, ISBN 5824-0)

Goliath At The Dog Show
Goliath helps David solve the mystery at the dog show—then gets a special prize for his effort! (Paperback, ISBN 3818-5—Library Binding, ISBN 5821-6)

Goliath's Christmas
Goliath plays a big part in rescuing a snowstorm victim. Then he and David join friends for the best Christmas party ever. (Paperback, ISBN 3878-9—Library Binding, ISBN 5843-7)

Goliath's Easter Parade
With important help from Goliath, David finds a way to save the neighborhood playground by raising funds at the Easter Parade. (Paperback, ISBN 3957-2—Library Binding, ISBN 5877-1)

Written by Terrance Dicks and illustrated by Valerie Littlewood, all Goliath books at bookstores. Or order direct from Barron's. Paperbacks $2.95 each, Library Bindings $7.95 each. When ordering direct from Barron's, please indicate ISBN number and add 10% postage and handling (Minimum $1.50). N.Y. residents add sales tax.

P.O. Box 8040, 250 Wireless Boulevard, Hauppauge, NY 11788
Call toll free: 1-800-645-3476, in NY 1-800-257-5729